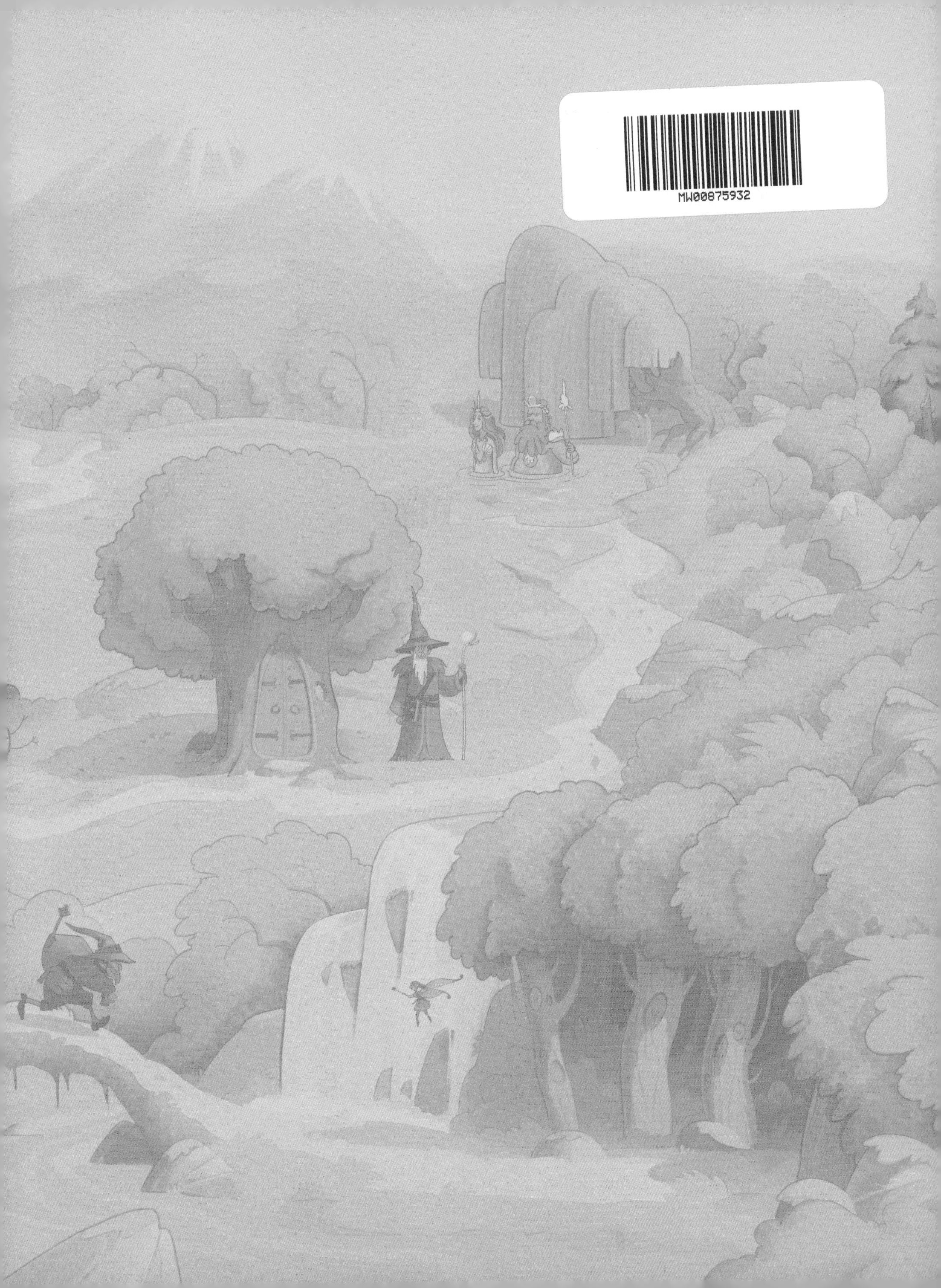

For my daughters, Audrey and Violet,
whose imagination inspires me every day.
Never stop dreaming.

**www.mascotbooks.com**

*The Search for the Scepter*

©2020 Julie Dinges. All Rights Reserved. No part of this publication may be reproduced, stored in a retrieval system or transmitted in any form by any means electronic, mechanical, or photocopying, recording or otherwise without the permission of the author.

**For more information, please contact:**
Mascot Books
620 Herndon Parkway, Suite 320
Herndon, VA 20170
info@mascotbooks.com

Library of Congress Control Number: 2020904176

CPSIA Code: PRT0320A
ISBN-13: 978-1-64543-008-7

Printed in the United States

# THE
# Search
## FOR THE
# Scepter

### JULIE DINGES

ILLUSTRATED BY
### NAZAR HOROKHIVSKYI

Princesses Rosalie and Scarlet awoke to a crash.
A thief had broken in and shattered the library window's glass.

Knights delivered sad news:
The king's scepter had been taken!
The royal family was completely
stunned and shaken.

The king and queen cried, "Whatever shall we do?"
Little did they know Rosalie and Scarlet had found a clue…

Yellow grains of sand, so tiny and teeny—
it could only mean the thief had fled to the genies!

The journey would be scary, but their mission was clear:
The scepter they'd find, and no thief they'd fear!

Into the forest
the brave princesses ran,
to the giant maple tree
that grew in the sand.

They jumped into the sand
and sunk right down
until they met a genie
walking his hound.

"A thief?" Spiro the genie said, consulting his pet.
"We saw one, yes, how could we forget?

He came through, dropping jewels in his wake,
but he's long gone! I believe he was heading for
Mermaid Lake."

The genie's hound, Tucker, barked his goodbyes to the girls,
as Spiro collected the thief's abandoned pearls.

At Mermaid Lake, a whirlpool led to the undersea.
Rosalie jumped in and shouted to Scarlet, "Follow me!"

They swam down, straight to the mermaid palace.
Thankfully they could breathe—what wondrous magic!

At the palace they were greeted with knowing and helpful eyes,
warning the sisters of distractions, diversions, and lies.

The mermaids said, "He swam so fast,
we couldn't quite catch the thief.
Though we did hear him whisper
about wizards as he passed Dolphin Reef.

So, to the home of the wizards you must go.
You must find the scepter, this you know."

The princesses curtsied and thanked the mermaids for their advice,
then swam to the surface and found a meadow of violets, purple and nice.

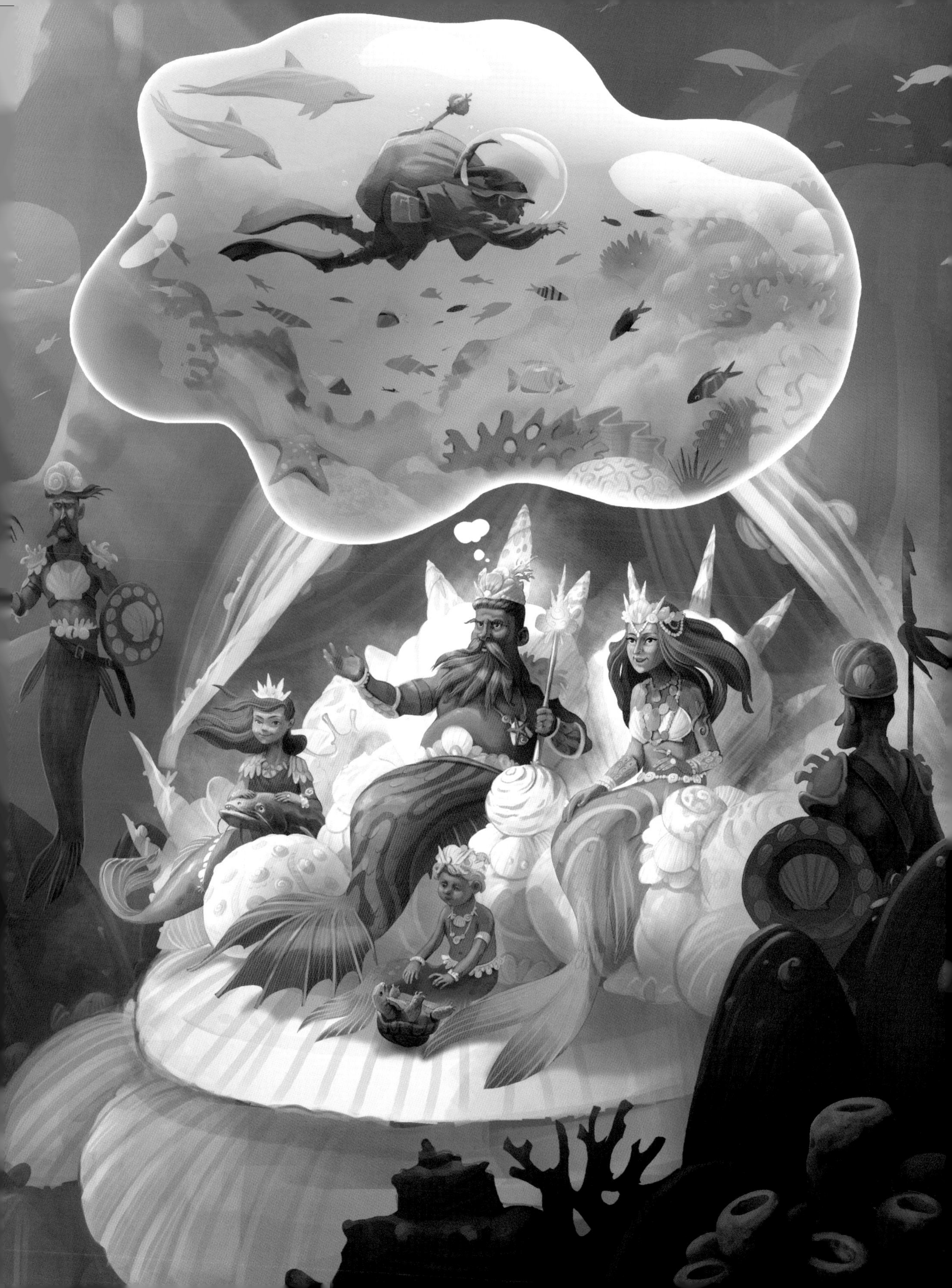

Beyond the meadow, they spied the enchanted door to the wizard's home,
and after answering a few riddles, it opened with a low, rumbling groan.

The magical men and women greeted the princesses
and were upset by their news.
"Who'd dare steal the king's scepter?" they shouted.
"Such an artifact we cannot lose.

A thief did come through here, but managed to avoid the spells we casted.
Though we did notice how he was becoming terribly flabbergasted.

He must be the same thief you both are chasing,
which explains his terrified look, knowing the fate he is facing.

He muttered something
under his breath about a shiny horn,
which could mean only one thing—
his next stop was the unicorns!"

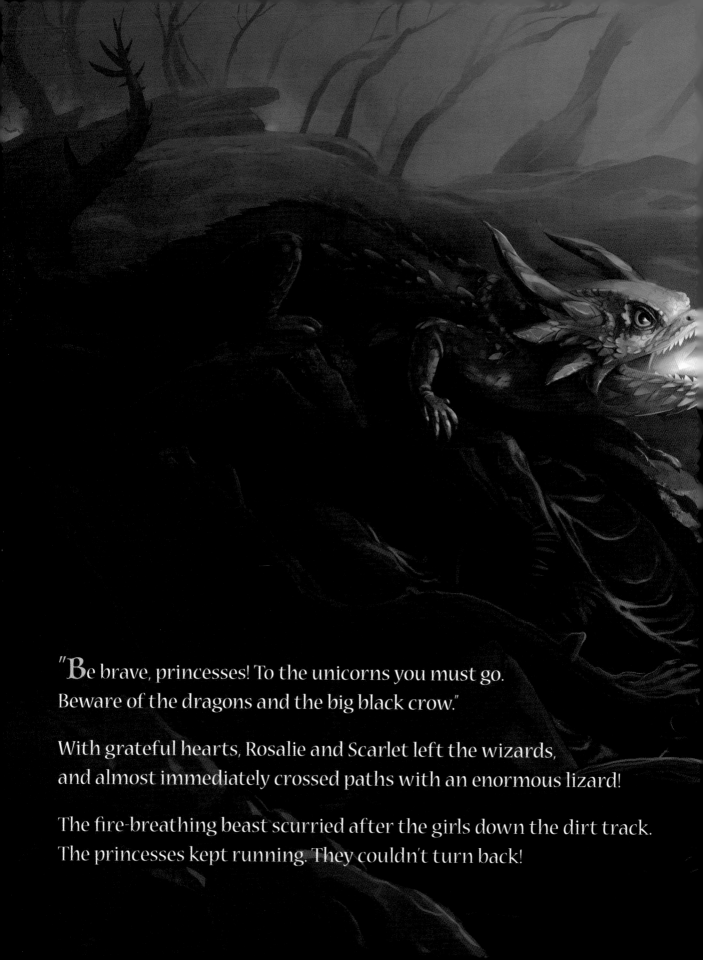

"Be brave, princesses! To the unicorns you must go.
Beware of the dragons and the big black crow."

With grateful hearts, Rosalie and Scarlet left the wizards,
and almost immediately crossed paths with an enormous lizard!

The fire-breathing beast scurried after the girls down the dirt track.
The princesses kept running. They couldn't turn back!

Jumping and maneuvering, they barely slipped by
and hoped their next stop had no dragons in the sky.

Deep in the forest
they found the unicorn's lair,
where they were received
by three most fair.

The girls thought, *How pretty
are these magical creatures!
Their sparkling horns, long manes,
and beautiful features.*

But they couldn't stay long—they had an important task,
so Scarlet stepped up, cleared her throat, and asked,

"We're following a thief who stole
the scepter from our father the king.
We need to find him and take the scepter home,
have you seen anything?"

"We did see your thief," the unicorns said.
"He dropped a golden arrow
that only warrior centaurs carry
when protecting the tree sparrows."

The princesses said their thanks
to the beautiful trio,
and pushed onward,
hoping to catch their foe.

In their forest sanctuary, the centaurs greeted their two royal guests
with a bowl of fresh berries as Rosalie told them of their quest.

"We saw your thief," they said. "You've just missed him.
He didn't stay long, for he knew his fate here would be grim.

He ran from us down that dark and tree-dense trail
toward the land of the fairies. Hurry, you mustn't fail!"

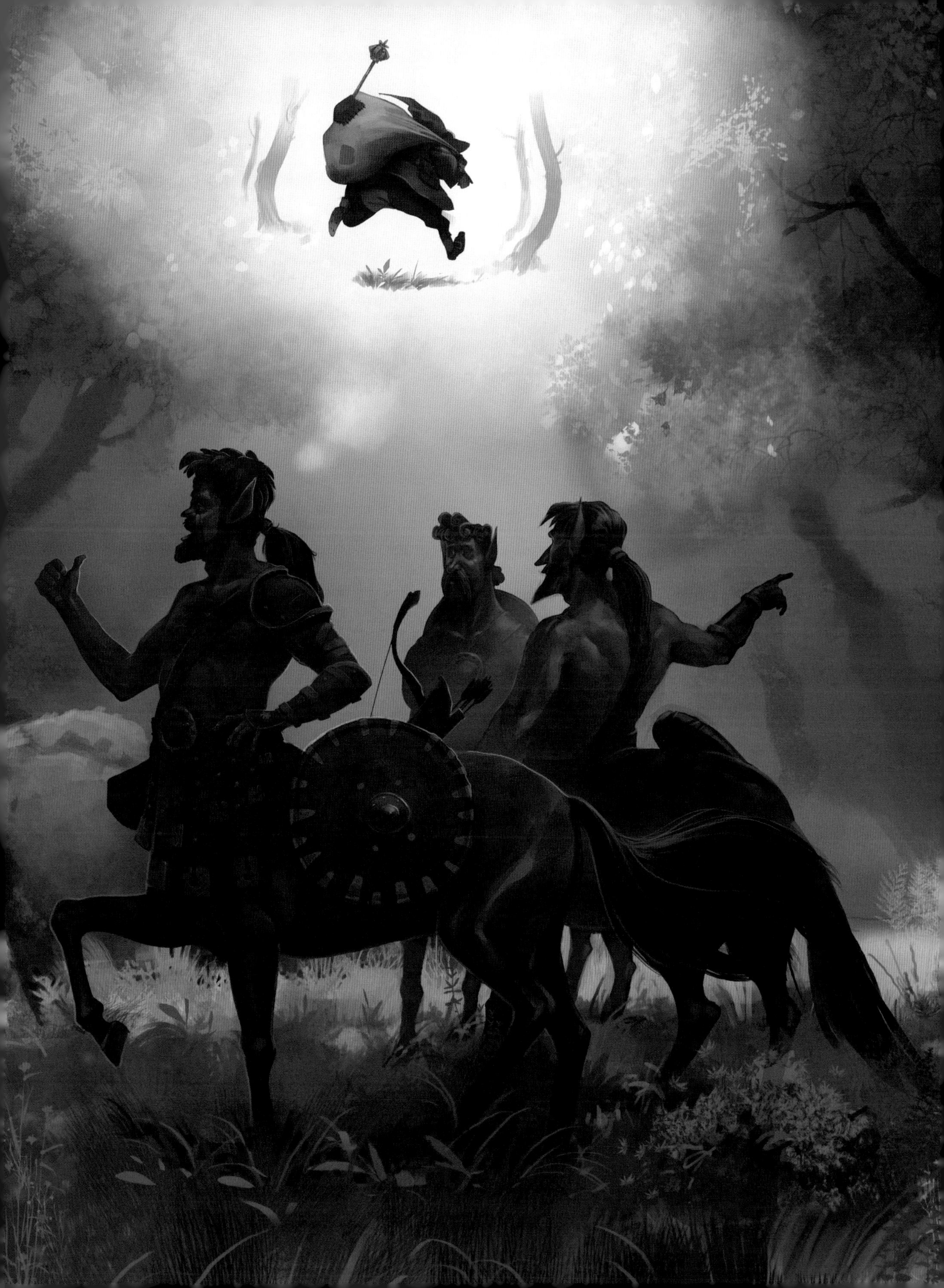

Tired and dirty from their seemingly endless mission,
they followed the dark, winding path.
Scarlet whispered to Rosalie, "When this is all over,
I'm taking a long, warm bubble bath."

At last, their trail came to an end
as they stepped out into the fairies' wooded glen.

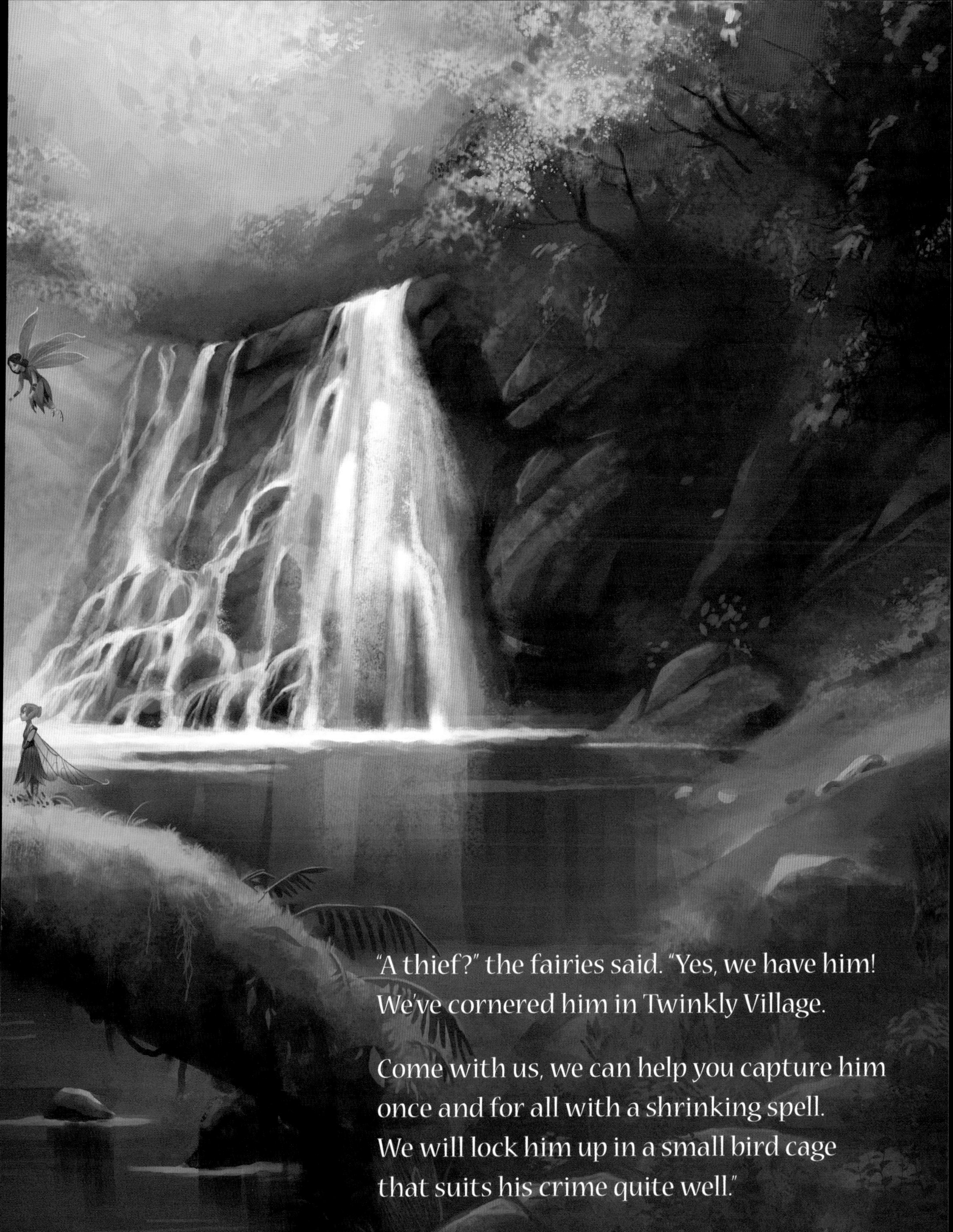

"A thief?" the fairies said. "Yes, we have him!
We've cornered him in Twinkly Village.

Come with us, we can help you capture him
once and for all with a shrinking spell.
We will lock him up in a small bird cage
that suits his crime quite well."

The princesses followed the fairies to the thief, who was quite irate.
Scarlet yelled out, "Finally thief, we have sealed your fate!"

Rosalie opened the bird cage door—they would trap the thief inside,
while Scarlet blocked his only exit so he couldn't run and hide.

Cast your spell!" the princesses said. "We've set our trap!"
The fairies' spell hit the thief true with a *zaaaap!*

"Curses!" the thief shouted as he dropped the scepter and shrank four times his size. Rosalie grabbed the stolen scepter and locked the bird cage door with many knots and ties.

"We couldn't have done it
without your help,"
the grateful sisters said to
the small winged creatures.
Blushing from their compliment,
they smiled and agreed
they were really
fantastic seekers.

"The scepter is safe and you may
take it home," said the fairies.
"Your route back to the palace
will be led by our
beautiful canaries."

Finally home, the princesses returned the scepter to the king and queen.
In celebration, they threw the grandest party the kingdom had ever seen.

All of the realm rejoiced that the thief had been apprehended.
Rosalie and Scarlet were happy their extraordinary adventure had ended.

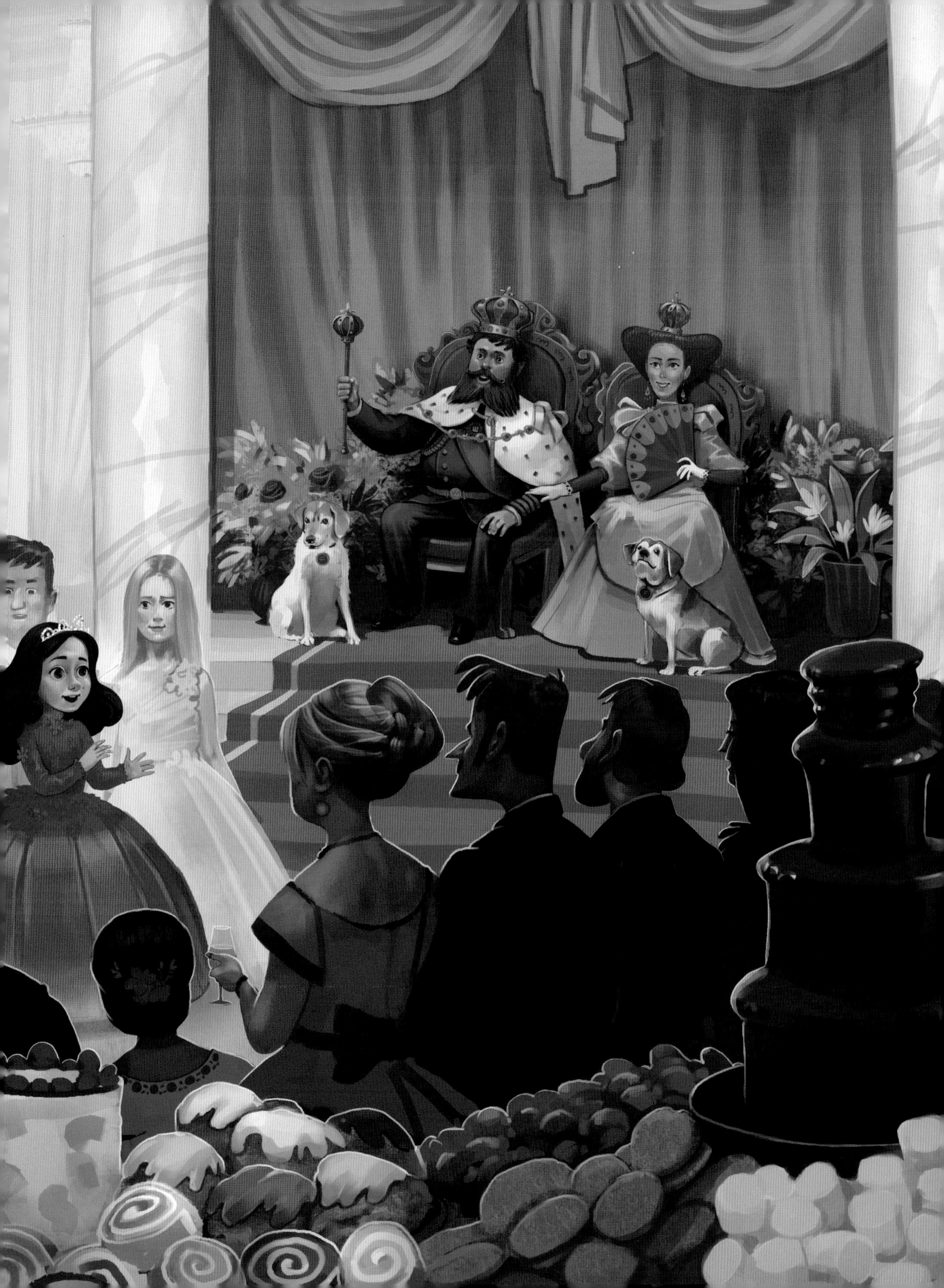

The story is over, but you may explore more and recap.
Turn the page and discover the magical lands from the princesses' map.

Sandy Maple

Unicorn Lair

Centaur Sanctuary

THE Search FOR THE Scepter

Mermaid Lake

Wizard Treehouse

Twinkly Village

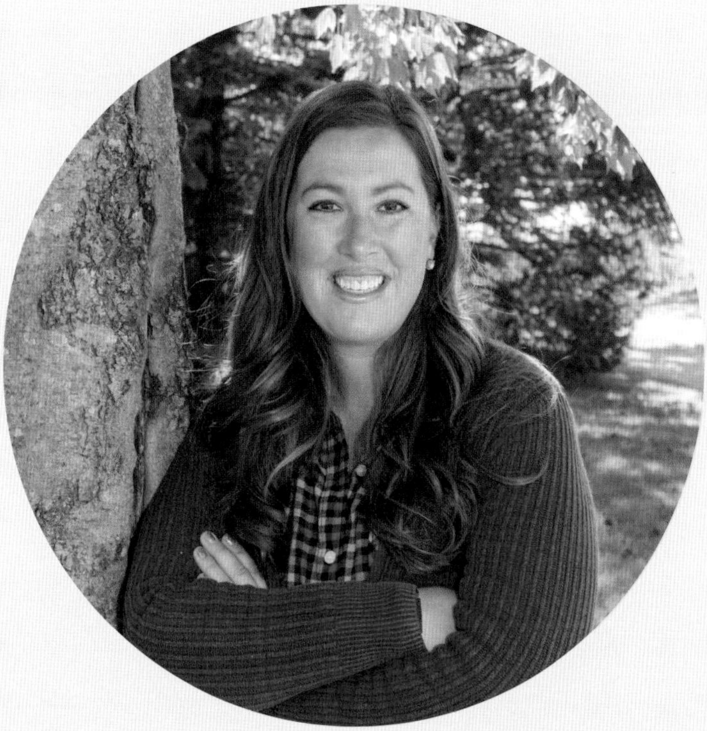

**Julie Dinges** lives in Hilliard, Ohio, with her husband, two daughters, one dog, and several fish. She loves being outside, cooking, traveling, watching science fiction movies, and reading fantasy books to her girls. Julie spent many years as a technical writer before shifting focus to website design.

One of Julie's greatest ambitions was to write a book. She is excited to share her first published creation, and hopes it sparks imagination and inspiration for all who read of the princesses' quest.

JULIEDINGES.COM

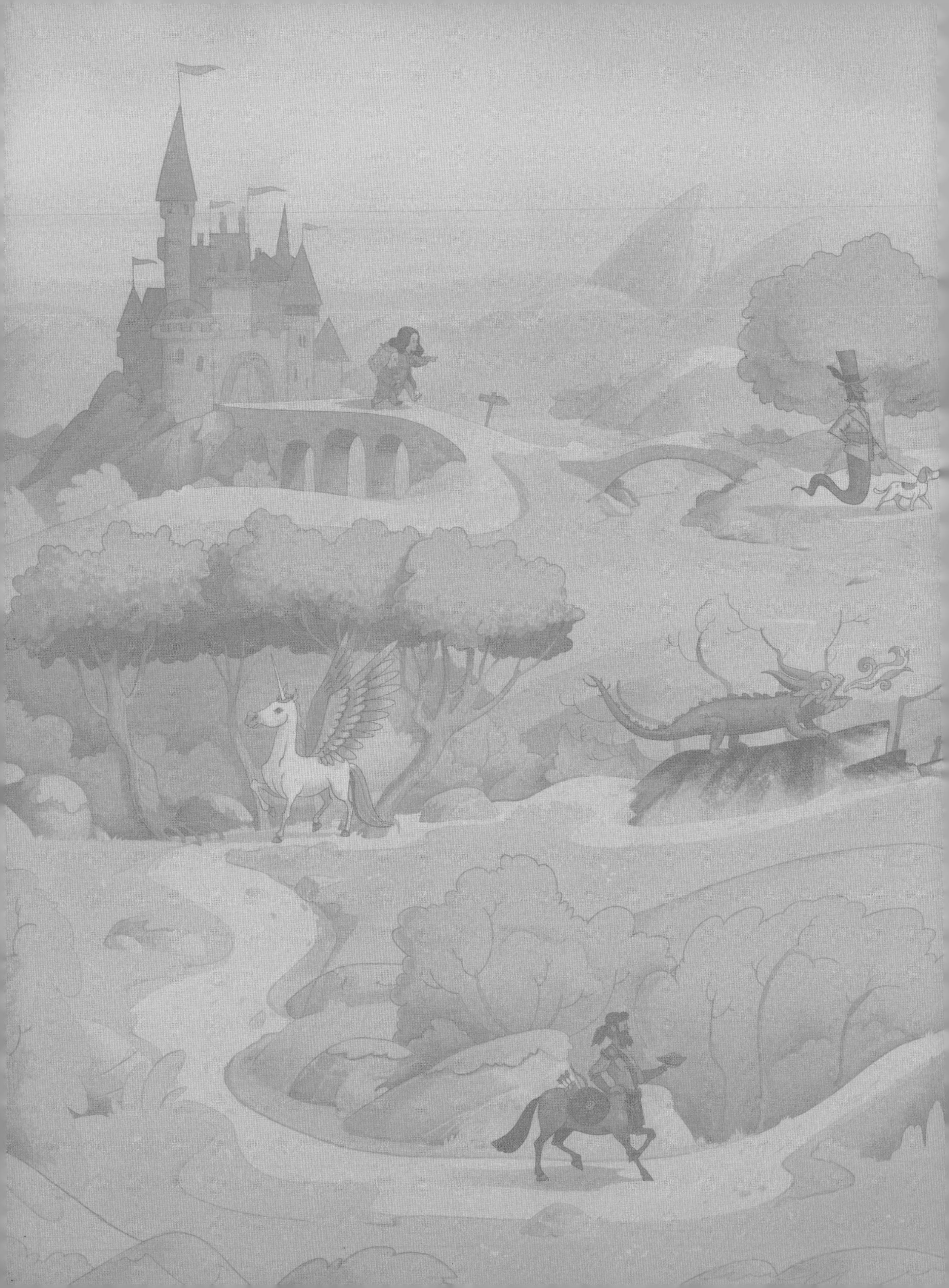